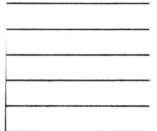

CALICO ILLUSTRATED CLASSICS

Charles Dickens's

David Copperfield

ADAPTED BY: Jan Fields
ILLUSTRATED BY: Howard McWilliam

magic Wagon

visit us at www.abdopublishing.com

Published by Magic Wagon, a division of the ABDO Group,
8000 West 78th Street, Edina, Minnesota 55439. Copyright
© 2011 by Abdo Consulting Group, Inc. International copyrights
reserved in all countries. All rights reserved. No part of this
book may be reproduced in any form without written permission
from the publisher.

Calico Chapter Books™ is a trademark and logo of Magic Wagon.

Printed in the United States of America, Melrose Park, Illinois.
052010
092010
This book contains at least 10% recycled materials.

Original text by Charles Dickens
Adapted by Jan Fields
Illustrated by Howard McWilliam
Edited by Stephanie Hedlund and Rochelle Baltzer
Cover and interior design by Abbey Fitzgerald

Library of Congress Cataloging-in-Publication Data

Fields, Jan.
  Charles Dickens's David Copperfield / adapted by Jan Fields ;
illustrated by Howard McWilliam.
      p. cm. -- (Calico illustrated classics)
  ISBN 978-1-60270-745-0
  [1. Orphans--Fiction. 2. Coming of age--Fiction. 3. Great Britain--
History--19th century--Fiction.] I. McWilliam, Howard, 1977- ill. II.
Dickens, Charles, 1812-1870. David Copperfield. III. Title. IV. Title:
David Copperfield.
  PZ7.F479177Ch 2010
  [Fic]--dc22
                                    2010003919

Table of Contents

CHAPTER 1: I Am Born 4

CHAPTER 2: I Have a Change 9

CHAPTER 3: I Am Sent Away 16

CHAPTER 4: Salem House 22

CHAPTER 5: My Holiday 28

CHAPTER 6: A Memorable Birthday 33

CHAPTER 7: Life on My Own 39

CHAPTER 8: My Aunt Makes Up Her Mind
about Me 44

CHAPTER 9: Another Beginning 52

CHAPTER 10: I Am a New Boy 59

CHAPTER 11: Somebody Turns Up 63

CHAPTER 12: I Choose a Profession 69

CHAPTER 13: A Loss 75

CHAPTER 14: My Aunt Astonishes Me 80

CHAPTER 15: Dora's Aunts 89

CHAPTER 16: Intelligence 96

CHAPTER 17: The New Wound 104

CHAPTER 18: A Light Shines 108

I Am Born

I have been told that I was born on a Friday at midnight. I was born in the small town of Blunderstone in Suffolk, England. My father had died some six months before.

The most surprising thing about my birth was the visitor who arrived just before it. Betsey Trotwood was my father's aunt. Miss Trotwood had once been married. Her husband was a great disappointment to her, considering he once tried to toss her out of a third-story window. She paid him off, and he went away to India. Miss Trotwood then lived as a single woman for the rest of her life. She believed strongly that all women would benefit from life without husbands.

On the afternoon before my arrival, my mother was sitting by the fire. She was missing my father and fretting that she would not survive my arrival. At some point, my mother's eyes drifted toward the window. There she saw a strange lady with her nose pressed to the window.

My mother jumped from her chair as Miss Trotwood strode in. "Mrs. David Copperfield, I think?" the older woman inquired.

"Yes," my mother whispered just before bursting into tears.

"Oh, tut, tut," Miss Trotwood said. "Don't do that!"

But my mother had little choice and did cry until she had quite cried herself out. Miss Trotwood demanded to know the name of my mother's servant. Then, she opened the parlor door and shouted, "Here, Peggotty! Tea. Your mistress is a little unwell. Don't dawdle."

Then Miss Trotwood sat and announced, "Your child will be a girl. I am certain. From the moment of her birth, I will be her friend and her godmother. I would like you to name her Betsey Trotwood Copperfield."

My mother was so awed by Miss Trotwood that she didn't dare argue the point. But she did burst into a fresh storm of tears.

"Well," my aunt said. "Don't cry anymore. You'll make yourself ill. And it won't be good for you or my goddaughter."

Her firm instance seemed to do my mother some good, for she did stop crying. Peggotty carried in the tea things and took one look at my mother before sending word for the doctor. Miss Trotwood merely stuffed bits of cotton in her ears and waited by the fire.

The doctor arrived quickly and saw to my mother. As I was still some hours away from arrival, he came downstairs to warm by the fire. Seeing the cotton in my aunt's ears, he assumed she had an earache and offered some medical advice for curing it.

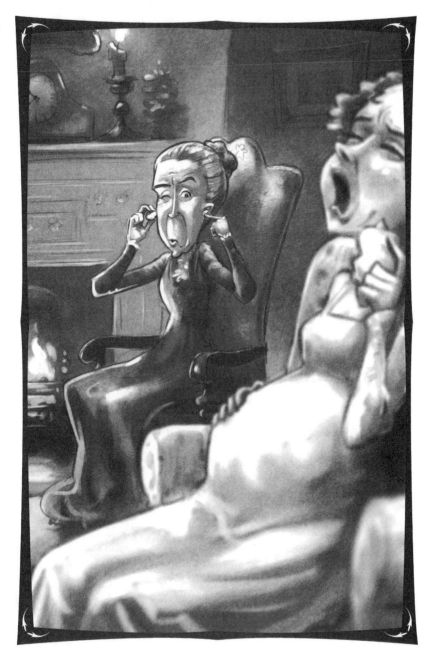

"Nonsense," Miss Trotwood snapped so firmly that the doctor made no other attempt at conversation. He went up and down the stairs several times to check on my mother. Each time he came into the parlor, my aunt glared at him until he slunk upstairs again.

Finally the doctor came down and said, "I am happy to congratulate you."

"How is she?" my aunt asked.

"As comfortable as she can be after such a task," he said. "You may see her presently. It might do her some good."

My aunt waved this speech away and leaned closer to the doctor. "And she. How is she?"

The doctor stared at her blankly.

"The baby?" Miss Trotwood finally prompted.

The doctor said with a smile, "He is a healthy boy."

My aunt said nothing. She merely turned around and walked out. She never came back.

I Have a Change

My memories of my own early years were pleasant. I can clearly picture my mother's pretty hair and our dear Peggotty's apple-red cheeks. My mother and Peggotty spoiled me completely, and I was happy to imagine the three of us alone forever.

Still my mother too soon began walking home from church on the arm of a tall gentleman named Murdstone. The man called me a prince and my mother laughed. I did not like him or the way he touched my mother's arm.

Eventually I learned I would have a two-week outing to visit some of Peggotty's relatives in Yarmouth. It sounded like a grand adventure and I looked forward to it totally.

When the day arrived to leave, the carrier's cart waited at the gate. My mother kissed me so fondly that I cried at the thought of leaving her and home. She cried a little too and hugged me for a long moment.

When the cart rolled on, I looked back to see my mother standing in the road. Mr. Murdstone came to stand beside her and scolded her. I wondered what business it was of his to scold my mother! I turned to look at Peggotty and saw a frown on her face to match my own.

After this, I quickly turned my attention to the adventure ahead. The carrier's horse walked slowly. We spent much of the ride either dozing or eating snacks from a great basket Peggotty carried.

Finally we reached Yarmouth. I thought the place spongy and soppy and amazingly flat.

The small village smelled of fish, pitch, and tar. The streets were crowded with sailors and carts.

I jumped nearly off my seat when Peggotty shouted, "Here's my Ham!"

Amazingly, she was not talking about a breakfast meat, but a tall boy with curly light hair like a sheep. He took me on his back and carried me along through the crowds. We headed quickly through the village and back out onto the flat, spongy wasteland.

"Yon's our house, Mas'r Davy," Ham said.

I looked in all directions but couldn't see a single house. I saw flat land, river, and an old boat pulled up onto the land.

"Is that it?" I asked. "The ship-looking thing?"

"That's it, Mas'r Davy."

I could imagine nothing more wonderful than living on a ship, even one hauled out of the water. It was very clean and tidy inside with pleasant framed pictures on the walls. Most of the seating was made from boxes and lockers.

Peggotty opened a little door and showed me my bedroom. It had a little window where the rudder once passed through. The room held a little bed with a bright patchwork quilt and a tiny table with a handful of seaweed displayed in a blue mug.

I then met the most beautiful little girl I had ever seen. She giggled and ran whenever I came close to her. Her name was Emily. Then, Peggotty called me over to meet the scruffy, smiling man who was her brother.

"Glad to see you, sir," said Mr. Peggotty. "We're proud of your company."

I learned that neither Ham nor the pretty little Emily were Mr. Peggotty's children. They were orphans whose fathers had drowned, but it was clear that Mr. Peggotty had as much affection for them as any father.

"Have you any children?" I asked.

"No," he answered with a laugh. "I've never been married."

I leaned close and pointed to the glum lady in the apron who sat knitting by the fire. "Then who is that?"

"That's Mrs. Gummidge."

That was all that was said on the matter at that time. I later learned that Mrs. Gummidge was the widow of Mr. Peggotty's partner. As she was very poor, he had taken her in.

"My brother is as good as gold and as true as steel," Peggotty said. And I never had reason to doubt it.

I spent most of my stay playing with Emily, and we soon became the very closest of friends. I was certain that I loved her and we would grow up someday to be married.

I learned both Ham and Mr. Peggotty worked very hard and never had a hard word or a sour face. The same could not be said of Mrs. Gummidge, who never smiled once during my visit.

"I'm a lone creature," she moaned at least once a day. This announcement puzzled me.

Certainly she seemed forlorn, as I had never seen a gloomier creature. But she lived in the middle of such a cheery family that I could not see why she thought herself alone.

No matter how hard anyone tried to cheer her, she would only sink deeper into gloom. But even her gloomy announcements could not dull my pleasure in the visit.

Too soon, the time came to go home. When we arrived back at our own dear house, my mother did not come out to meet us.

"Where is she?" I cried, suddenly terrified that my mother had died.

"She is inside," Peggotty said and gave me a quick hug. "With your new Pa."

I trembled and turned white. "I don't want to see him."

But Peggotty led me straight to the best parlor, where my mother sat on one side of the fire and Mr. Murdstone sat on the other. When she would have run to me, Mr. Murdstone scolded her and we had to settle for a kiss on the cheek.

As soon as I could creep away, I did. I found my bedroom moved to a tiny room far from the others. I was home, but home was no more.

I Am Sent Away

Eventually I cried myself to sleep in my little bed. I awoke to find my mother and Peggotty had come to look for me. They fussed over me until a stern voice spoke from behind them.

"Clara, have you forgotten? Firmness, my dear!" said Mr. Murdstone.

"I am very sorry, Edward," my mother said. "I meant to be very good."

My stepfather drew her to him, whispered in her ear, and kissed her. "Go below, my love," he said. "David and I will come down together." My mother and Peggotty left.

"David, do you know what I do with a stubborn dog?" Mr. Murdstone asked.

"I don't know," I answered.

"I beat him."

And with that, I learned my place in the household. I was no longer the favored son. I was now the focus of lessons in firmness for my gentle mother. I became the stick that my stepfather used to beat my mother every time she turned a kind look or soft word my way.

It was not long after this that we added another Murdstone to the house. Mr. Murdstone's sister came to live with us. She had the same cold viciousness of her brother. Her first declaration over me was, "Wants manners." That was the highest praise I ever received from her.

Before the Murdstones arrived, I was considered bright. I loved to read and had a keen interest in almost everything. But my stepfather decided my lessons had been too easy and my mother's hand too soft. So, each day I was given a great pile of lessons to learn and recite.

Whenever I faltered or misspoke, the Murdstones used it as an excuse to criticize my mother's teaching. Knowing that every mistake cost my mother soon turned me into a complete idiot.

"Be firm with the boy!" Mr. Murdstone thundered.

"Give him the book and make him know it," Miss Murdstone insisted.

I believe now that even with such heavy and tiresome lesson books, I would have made a fine showing of myself if not for the glares and snarls of the Murdstones. Finally, after endless days of my trying and failing, I came downstairs to discover Mr. Murdstone held a cane.

"I tell you, Clara," he said, "I was often beaten as a boy."

My mother looked near fainting as she stared at the cane. My own eyes strayed to it frequently and my lessons began badly and grew worse. Finally, my mother burst into tears.

"David, you and I will go upstairs," Mr. Murdstone said. "You will burden your mother no more today."

He walked me up to my room slowly and gravely. Once in my room, he grabbed my arm and struck me with the cane. At that, I twisted around and bit him fiercely on the hand that held me.

This was my first and only beating from Mr. Murdstone. I was locked in my room while plans were made. One afternoon, Peggotty rushed up the stairs to speak to me through the door.

"Is Mama very angry with me?" I asked.

I heard Peggotty crying softly on her side of the keyhole. "No. Not very."

"What is going to be done with me? Do you know?" I asked.

"School near London. You will leave tomorrow." Then Peggotty began to cry again. Finally she said, "I'll take care of your mama. And I'll write to you, my precious Davy."

"Thank you," I whispered.

The next morning, my things were loaded on the carrier's cart. Miss Murdstone watched my mother to see that she showed me no kindness. My stepfather was not around and I did not miss him.

When the cart rolled past our home, it rumbled again to a stop. Peggotty dashed from the bushes and handed me a stiff purse. Then she disappeared back to our house, never having said a word.

The purse held bright coins and a note in my mother's writing, "For Davy, with my love." I cried for a time, then wiped my nose with my pocket handkerchief and looked around me. Mr. Barkis, the driver, invited me to sit up beside him, so I climbed up.

"Will you be taking me all the way to London?" I asked.

"That horse would be deader than pork before we got halfway to London," he said, pointing toward his slow horse that plodded before us. "I'll take you to Yarmouth, where you'll catch a carriage."

I offered Mr. Barkis one of the cakes that Peggotty had packed for my ride and he ate it in one gulp. "Did she make them?" he asked.

"Peggotty?" I asked. "Yes, she makes all our pastry and does all our cooking."

He seemed to think about this for a long while and finally he asked, "Does she have a sweetheart?"

"No. She never had a sweetheart."

Another long while passed without conversation.

"If you'll be writin' to her," he said finally, "you could tell her that Barkis is willing."

"Just that message?" I said. "Barkis is willing."

He nodded. "Yes, Barkis is willing."

I agreed, though I had no idea the point of the message. We rode the rest of the way in companionable silence while I wondered what lay ahead.

Salem House

The change of coach went smoothly enough, though I found my next seventeen-hour ride less than comfortable. I was squished between two large gentlemen and nearly smothered when they both fell asleep and leaned toward me on each side.

By the time we reached London, I was hungry and exhausted. I found no one waited for me at the station. All kinds of imaginary fates skipped through my head before a gaunt young man with hollow cheeks and a black beard finally arrived to take me to school. Mr. Mell was one of my new schoolmasters.

The school itself was a grim brick building surrounded by a high wall. A man with a surly face and a wooden leg let us in the battered door in the wall.

Mr. Mell led me to an empty classroom. When I asked where the other boys were, he explained that the whole school had gone home for holiday time.

I looked around the dirty room and wrinkled my nose at the smell of moldy fabric and rotten apples. I walked through the long row of desks until I came to a beautifully lettered sign lying on a desk. It said, "Take care of him. He bites."

I scrambled up on the nearest desk and looked around in case a mad dog was lurking in the dim corners of the room. Mr. Mell asked why I was on a desk.

"I am looking for the dog," I said.

"Dog?" he echoed. "What dog?"

"The one that must be taken care of," I said. "The one that bites."

Mr. Mell looked very sad then. "That's not a dog, Copperfield. That's a boy. My instructions are to put that sign on your back."

He handed me down from the desk and hung the sign on my back like a knapsack. I was terribly embarrassed and tried to hide the sign whenever I could in the days ahead. Whenever the cruel man with the wooden leg spotted me, he would shout, "You, sir! Copperfield! Show that sign or I'll report you!"

Mr. Mell was never harsh with me. We passed the days until the return of the other boys in quiet lessons. I found these lessons much superior to the teaching of the Murdstones but not nearly as good as those from my own dear mother.

At the end of the holiday, the first person I met was the head of the school, Mr. Creakle. He announced that he admired my stepfather. I could see no good coming to me from that and none did.

Mr. Creakle was fond of pinching, smacking, and hitting boys with his cane. He often entered our classroom and struck students at random. The only good point to the man was that he found my sign got in the way of smacking me and soon had it discarded.

One of Creakle's favorite targets for beatings was Tommy Traddles, who was my first friend at school. Traddles introduced me to each of the other boys in turn. I quickly felt I was part of the group.

Most of these children blur in my memory but for Tommy and J. Steerforth. Steerforth was six years older than me and considered an amazing scholar. I thought him quite good looking and admired him tremendously.

"What money do you have, Copperfield?" Steerforth asked on meeting me.

"Seven shillings."

"You should let me look after your money," he said. "If you like."

I handed it over quickly and he recommended I spend some on sweets and drinks. Before I knew it, my entire fortune was spent on treats. We had a grand party in the moonlight of our dormitory and I felt honored to share with my new friends.

Though Creakle lashed every boy at some time or other, he never touched Steerforth. Steerforth insisted it was because Creakle was afraid of what he might do.

"What would you do?" one of the youngest boys asked.

"I'd knock him down," Steerforth said. "And that would be just the beginning."

We never doubted for a moment that our hero would do just exactly that. My admiration for Steerforth dimmed only once, when he provoked a needless argument with Mr. Mell and got the kind young teacher fired. I was completely confused to see my hero do such a shoddy thing.

"Don't worry about him," Steerforth assured us. "You know I'll write home and take care that Mr. Mell gets some money." This redeemed him completely in my eyes.

The good-natured friendship of Tommy Traddles and surprising support of Steerforth were the high points of my school days. The lessons were poorly taught, the food was dreadful, yet I still preferred it to a single moment with my new stepfather or his dreadful sister.

CHAPTER
5

My Holiday

About halfway through the school year, I was called from class with an announcement that I had visitors. I trudged to the dining room, expecting that the Murdstones had come to see that I was being taught in the most firm, horrible manner possible.

Instead I discovered Mr. Peggotty and Ham! I was so surprised and delighted, I burst into tears.

"Cheer up, Mas'r Davy," Ham said. "Why, how you have growed!"

"Am I grown?" I asked, drying my eyes.

Ham and his uncle agreed so loudly on my growth that they began laughing at one another and that made me laugh. They told me that

Peggotty and my mother were well. And they passed along greetings from Emily and Mrs. Gummidge.

While we were chatting, Steerforth came in. He greeted my friends with such enthusiasm that I was doubly proud to show him off.

We all got on so well, I promised to bring Steerforth along when I came to visit Yarmouth again. The rest of the school year moved along swiftly and finally holiday time came. I rather expected that I would be spending the time alone at school, but I learned I was to head home.

The trip back to our village was relatively uneventful, though the driver frowned and grunted instead of speaking.

"I wrote to Peggotty," I told Mr. Barkis. "I gave your message."

"Nothing come of it," he said gruffly. "No answer."

"You were expecting an answer?" I said.

"A man does."

"She might not know," I said. "I could tell her."

He seemed to think that a grand idea. The rest of the ride was made in decidedly better cheer. When we finally reached the house, I leaned against the door, afraid to open it. How welcome would I be in my own home?

Finally, I slipped softly into the house and discovered my lovely mother sitting by the fire with a tiny baby in her arms. When she saw me, she cried and kissed me and called me her own dear Davy. Then she showed me the tiny baby.

"He is your brother," she said. Then she kissed me again and hugged me. Peggotty must have heard the sounds, for she came running in and I was greeted all over again.

I learned that the Murdstones were off to visit friends and weren't due home before night. We had a lovely quiet family time until their arrival blew ice into the room again.

For the rest of my visit, my mother was berated for any kind word she turned toward me. I was forbidden to move too near my new baby brother. When I tried to slip away to my room so that my mother would not be scolded on my behalf, I was forbidden.

"I observe you have a sullen disposition," Mr. Murdstone announced.

"Sulky as a bear," Miss Murdstone added.

"I have not meant to be sullen, sir," I said, hoping to draw attention away from my mother.

"Don't lie!" Murdstone snapped. For the rest of the visit, he ordered me around like a dog and I obeyed like a dog. As much as I loved my mother and new baby brother, I felt relief when the holiday was over.

On the day I left, my mother ignored Miss Murdstone's sharp tone and kissed me good-bye and hugged me very tight. Then she stood with the baby and waved after the carrier cart until we were out of sight.

I never saw her again.

A Memorable Birthday

School passed quickly, and soon it was my birthday. I was on the playground when I got a call to come to the parlor. I assumed Peggotty had sent a hamper for my birthday.

I found Mr. Creakle in the parlor with his wife. "I am grieved to tell you," Mrs. Creakle said gently, "your mama is not well."

A mist rose between Mrs. Creakle and myself as my eyes filled with tears. I knew what she would say next. I read it on her face.

"She is dead and the baby, too."

I broke into a cry. Mrs. Creakle was very kind to me and helped me prepare to return home. I was to bring everything with me. The trip was a blur. Over and over, my mother's lovely face appeared in my thoughts.

I was deposited with the tailor and funeral furnisher to be prepared for the funeral. He told me my mother would be buried with the baby in her arms. Her stone would be beside that of my father.

The funeral was a quiet affair, as many of my mother's friends had been shut out of her life by the Murdstones. Still, it seemed forever before I could finally be alone with my own dear Peggotty.

"She was never well for a long time," Peggotty said gently. "Then after the baby was born, she just faded a little each day until she was gone."

The first thing Mr. Murdstone did after the funeral was give Peggotty a month's notice. Nothing was said about me, though it was clear I would not be returning to school.

"What will you do, Peggotty?" I asked.

"I will go to see my brother first," she said. "Perhaps they will let you come with me for a time."

As the Murdstones took no joy in seeing my face, they agreed that I might go. On the day of our leaving, Mr. Barkis was clearly delighted to be transporting Peggotty in his cart. He eyed her and asked, "Are you comfortable?"

She laughed and said she was.

"But really and truly, are you?" he growled, scooting closer to her and nearly squashing me in the seat between. When we finally arrived in Yarmouth, Mr. Barkis plucked at my sleeve and winked.

"It's all right," he whispered. "You made it all right first."

I found him completely confusing but I tried to nod wisely. Later Peggotty asked me what I might think of her getting married.

"As long as you liked me just as much," I said, "I would think it might be a good thing. Do you mean to marry Mr. Barkis?"

"Yes," said Peggotty.

"You would have a home and you could come and visit sometimes in his horse and cart," I said. "I think that would be good."

So Peggotty hugged me breathless and we hurried on to begin the visit with her brother. I found Mr. Peggotty not a bit changed and Mrs. Gummidge just as gloomy as last I saw her.

Emily had grown into a lovely young girl and seemed shy of me. She was clearly fascinated when her uncle asked me about Steerforth and I launched into tales of my good friend. I had a grand visit with only one surprise that came quite near to the end.

Peggotty and Mr. Barkis were set to go on a day's holiday together and Emily and I were to come along. Mr. Barkis wore a new blue coat. Mr. Peggotty threw a shoe after our departing cart for luck and we rolled away.

The first thing we did on our trip was stop at a church. Peggotty and Mr. Barkis went in alone as Emily and I waited in the cart. I told Emily then that I loved her, but she only laughed at me.

Finally, Mr. Barkis and Peggotty returned and we drove away into the country. Mr. Barkis turned to me with a wink and asked, "When I sent my message by you, what's the full name of the lass who heard it?"

I looked at him, puzzled. "Clara Peggotty."

"And what's her name now?"

"Clara Peggotty?"

"Clara Peggotty Barkis!" he said with a roar of laughter that shook the cart. They were married.

Later Peggotty said to me, "Young or old, Davy dear. You are welcome in my home for as long as you like or need. There will always be a place for you."

The next morning, I returned home. I was ignored by the Murdstones for some days until Mr. Murdstone called me downstairs.

"I have no interest in investing further in your education and see no value in it for a boy like you. But I believe you can be useful. Mr. Quinion works in one of my counting houses in London. He employs some boys, and he is willing to employ you."

"You will leave tomorrow," Miss Murdstone said. "Do your duty."

Thus, in the morning I was handed over to Mr. Quinion and we left for London.

Life on My Own

My job consisted of washing out wine bottles, pasting labels on full bottles, and packing them in casks. It was filthy, tiresome work in a gloomy warehouse. I was never mistreated and did not complain, but I was deeply ashamed to be given a task generally handed to beggars.

I was still a very small boy. People constantly stared to see me buying my own food and moving about the streets alone. I became quite used to it, though I sometimes found it difficult to get the attention of vendors.

The only high point in my existence was boarding with an unusual family by the name of Micawber.

Mr. Micawber spoke with a genteel air but seemed constantly on the edge of financial ruin. This teetering edge had an odd effect on his emotions. I had often seen him weeping with his wife over the certainty of ending up in debtor's prison, then hours later laughing over chops for dinner.

The door to their house wore a great brass plate that read "Mrs. Micawber's Boarding Establishment for Young Ladies." But I never saw a single young lady linger near the door.

The family treated me warmly and included me in everything they did, sometimes far more than they should. I heard about every unsettled bill and every disappointed plan or hope. Their kindness was all that carried me along as I labored each day at the wine bottles.

The Micawbers did an amazing job of hiding from creditors for months. But early one morning, Mr. Micawber was arrested and sent to the King's Bench Prison.

All the household furniture was sold and carried away in a van. Mrs. Micawber moved into the prison, where her husband had a room to himself.

I hired a little room outside the walls of the prison. I had grown too used to the Micawbers to part, and they seemed equally attached to me. We continued this way for months.

I entered the prison each morning as soon as the gates opened and ate my breakfast with the Micawbers. Mr. Micawber was much admired in the prison and his advice was sought out by many of the other prisoners. During this time, Mr. Micawber worked on a document that would secure his release.

As soon as they were free of the prison, the Micawbers decided to leave London. When that day grew close at hand, I found myself truly depressed. My job was shoddy and beneath me. My clothes were in tatters. And the closest thing I had to family was leaving.

As the Micawbers drove away, I realized I had only one answer to my problem. I would run away. I would find the only relation I had in the world, Miss Betsey Trotwood.

With this plan fixed, I decided to act on it immediately. I wrote a letter to Peggotty to ask if she knew where Miss Trotwood lived. I also asked if I might borrow a bit of money.

Peggotty's response came quickly and was full of her love, as always. She sent me the money I asked for, though I knew it must have been difficult to get such a sum from Mr. Barkis. He believed in extreme thriftiness. She told me that Miss Trotwood lived near Dover but that she knew nothing more specific.

I decided to set out at the end of that week. I wanted to be certain that I had worked off the full extent of my pay so that no one could argue I had stolen from them. Then on the last day, I simply left work with no intention of returning.

My first adventure, unfortunately, came when a long-legged young man stole my small box of belongings. My money from Peggotty was gone along with it. Thus, I left London with less than I had carried into it.

My Aunt Makes Up Her Mind about Me

As I trudged along, I discovered that I still had a few very small coins deep in my pocket. They would do little to feed me on my long walk to Dover, so the first thing I did was sell my vest for a sad few coins. I suspected my jacket would go next, but I resolved to keep it for a while as the nights were chilly.

I passed the first night's sleep in a haystack behind my old school. Fond memories of my school time kept me company through the night.

The next day was Sunday and I walked a full twenty-three miles by the end of the day. I ate a small loaf of bread I bought and slept on a patch of long grass. The steady tread of the night watchman past me lulled me to sleep and I felt quite safe.

The rest of my journey passed similarly. I was cheated a few times. Once a fierce young man threatened to beat me if I didn't give him my pocket handkerchief, so I did.

On the sixth day of my flight, I set foot in Dover. I was sunburned and very dirty. I met a kind-faced man and dared ask him whether he knew my aunt.

"Trotwood," he said, thoughtfully. "Old lady? Stiff in the back? Gruffish and sharp?"

I sadly nodded, thinking all these descriptions were likely.

"Follow the road up to the houses that face the sea. She lives up there somewhere," he said. "Someone should be able to direct you." Then he handed me a coin and headed on his way.

I bought a loaf of bread and felt much better for having it. Then I limped up the road. When

I reached the row of houses the man had described, I stepped into a shop and asked again about my aunt.

A young woman turned to me. "My mistress? What do you want with her?"

"I want to speak to her," I said. "Please."

"To beg from her probably," the young woman said with a sniff. She looked me over doubtfully, then said I should follow her. Finally, we reached a very neat little cottage with a garden full of flowers.

"This is Miss Trotwood's," the young woman said.

I walked hesitantly toward the house, suddenly aware of how very dirty and shabby I was. I glanced up and saw a pleasant-looking gentleman peering at me. He winked and nodded at me several times with a bright smile, then he backed away from the window.

I froze at that and could not find the courage to take another step. Suddenly, a lady wearing

gardening gloves and carrying a big knife stalked out of the house.

"Go away," she said, gesturing at me with the knife. "Go along! No boys here!"

"If you please, Aunt," I said, my voice as weak as water.

"Eh?"

"If you please, Aunt, I am your nephew. I am David Copperfield. My dear mama has died and I have been slighted and taught nothing and set to work not fit for me. I have run away. I was robbed and walked here from London." Then suddenly I broke into a passion of crying.

My aunt grabbed me and took me into the parlor. She opened a tall cupboard, took out several bottles, and dosed me with a bit from each of them. I am fairly certain she chose them at random as I tasted anchovy sauce and salad dressing. Then she had me lay on the sofa with a shawl and her own handkerchief under me to keep my clothes from dirtying the furniture.

I lay very still, too startled to know what to do. She rang a bell and I heard her say, "Janet, go upstairs and ask Mr. Dick to come here. I need him."

Janet seemed surprised to see me laid out stiffly on the sofa, but she went quickly on her errand. My aunt paced until the gentleman I had seen through the window came in.

"This," she said pointing toward me, "is David

Copperfield's son. He has run away. What shall we do with him?"

"Why if I was you," Mr. Dick said, "I should wash him!"

"Janet," said my aunt, turning to the servant, "Mr. Dick sets us all right. Heat the bath."

From my frozen place on the sofa I observed that my aunt was a handsome woman. She had very quick, bright eyes.

Mr. Dick had large gray eyes and his manner made me suspect his brain was a bit scrambled. He kept his head bowed, not by age but as if he'd been beaten and didn't quite dare hold his head up yet.

Janet was a pretty girl of about nineteen or twenty and very neat. I was beginning to settle down, when my aunt shouted, "Janet! Donkeys!"

This was the first battle of the donkeys that I would witness. Saddled donkeys were a popular mode of travel around the immediate area. My aunt allowed no donkeys to walk or feed upon the lush bit of green in front of the cottage. The boys who led the donkeys came to the patch of grass as often as possible. The battles were fierce and frequent.

After three donkey battles, my bath was ready and so comfortable I nearly fell asleep in the water. My aunt and Mr. Dick enrobed me in a shirt and pair of pants from his wardrobe tied up in shawls like a bundle of laundry. I soon lay down on the couch and fell asleep.

When I finally awoke, we dined and my aunt asked me a great many questions about my experiences. She listened quietly with only an occasional outburst of "Mercy upon us!"

When I had finished my tale, Aunt Betsey shook her head, "Whatever made that poor baby marry again? One would think his very name would put her off. Who would marry a murderer or one named like it? And then that Peggotty marries and leaves this child quite alone!"

I couldn't stand to hear a single harsh word said against my dear Peggotty. I jumped in to defend her as the dearest, truest nurse a child could ever have.

"Well," said my aunt. "The child is right to stand by those who have stood by him. Janet! Donkeys!"

After a brief skirmish, my aunt appealed to Mr. Dick again for advice as to what they should do with me.

"With David's son?" Mr. Dick said. "We should put him to bed."

And so they did.

Another Beginning

I fit into the household smoothly and soon was a great favorite of Mr. Dick. Apparently Mr. Dick was a distant relative of Miss Trotwood. He was considered quite mad by his family. He would have ended up in an asylum if not for Miss Trotwood. She took him in and his family paid a small stipend for his care.

Mr. Dick spent most of his day working on a book. He also had a tremendously large kite, written all over with remarks about King Charles the First. He promised I could help him fly it as soon as I had suitable clothes.

Early on, I learned that my aunt had written to my stepfather. I lived the next weeks in high anxiety about what would become of me.

At length a reply came from Mr. Murdstone. It said he would be coming to speak to my aunt himself the next day. And the next morning, two donkeys trod upon the patch of green bearing Mr. and Miss Murdstone.

My aunt rushed out to do battle and soon had the donkeys ejected and the Murdstones completely rumpled. Then Aunt Betsey marched into the house without greeting the Murdstones.

Aunt Betsey waited for Janet to announce the visitors. She insisted I remain in the room as she dealt with them. Then she called for Janet to bring Mr. Dick.

My aunt looked at the Murdstones sharply. "So, you are the Mr. Murdstone who married the widow of my late nephew David Copperfield?"

"I am," said Mr. Murdstone.

"It would have been a better thing if you'd left that poor girl alone," Aunt Betsey said.

"We are here to discuss this boy," Mr. Murdstone said. "He has a rebellious spirit, a violent temper, and an ungrateful nature."

"I believe this is the worst boy of all the boys in the world," Miss Murdstone said.

"Why are you helping him in his misbehavior?" Mr. Murdstone asked.

"Because you married his mother and worried her to death. Because you were a tyrant and you broke her heart. Because you took her property, left to her by my nephew. You gave no proper care to his son," Aunt Betsey began.

Miss Murdstone tried to interrupt, but my aunt ignored her completely. "You set him to work that was unfit and you behaved shabbily," my aunt continued. "I don't believe a word of what you have said about this boy."

"Miss Trotwood," Mr. Murdstone said as he rose, "if you were a gentleman—"

"Bah, stuff and nonsense. The boy will stay here unless he wishes to go with you." She turned to me and I begged her not to make me leave.

"In that case," my aunt said, turning back to the Murdstones, "good day, sir, and good-bye. Good day to you too, ma'am. If you ride a donkey on my green again, I'll knock your bonnet off and tread on it."

And so the Murdstones stormed out arm in arm.

Aunt Betsey turned to Mr. Dick. "We shall be guardians of this boy. We shall change his name to Trotwood Copperfield. Now what shall we do with him first?"

Mr. Dick looked me over solemnly and announced, "Get him some clothes!"

So they did and I began my new life in a new name. I felt like someone in a happy dream. Mr. Dick soon became my best friend and we went out often to fly the great kite.

My aunt treated me fondly as well. "Trot," she said one day. "We must not forget your education. Should you like to go to school in Canterbury?"

I replied that I would like it very much. My aunt and I left the next day. We went first to Canterbury to see Mr. Wickfield, who handled my aunt's legal affairs. He could be counted upon to recommend a suitable school.

We were greeted by a tall youth of about fifteen. His red hair was cropped to stubble and his eyes were an odd shade of reddish-brown like dried blood. He was bony and his black clothes made him seem all the more skeletal.

"Is Mr. Wickfield at home, Uriah Heep?" my aunt asked.

Uriah Heep admitted that his master was home and led us to a room where we met a gray-haired gentleman. My aunt told him that she wanted to send me to a school where I would be well treated and well taught. Mr. Wickfield knew just the school.

The only problem lay in where I would board. Finally, the lawyer said, "Leave your nephew here for the present. He's a quiet fellow and won't disturb me at all."

My aunt liked that offer and so did I. Mr. Wickfield showed us the living quarters above the offices. He introduced us to his housekeeper, his daughter Agnes. She had a bright, happy calmness about her that I shall never forget.

My aunt was well content with the household and the school. She finally turned to me and said, "Trot, be a credit to yourself, to me, and to Mr. Dick."

I promised as well as I could and thanked her repeatedly. She gave me a quick hug before she left.

I settled into the house quickly and came to three conclusions: I liked Agnes very much, I disliked Uriah Heep in equal measure, and I worried for the great quantity of wine Mr. Wickfield drank each evening. It didn't seem wise. In these three things, my mind only became more set over time.

CHAPTER
10

I Am a New Boy

The next morning, Mr. Wickfield walked me to my new school and introduced me to its master, Doctor Strong. The doctor was a rusty-looking older man with a slightly distracted air. He took us to the large schoolroom in the quietest side of the house.

About twenty-five boys were reading at the desks when we entered. They rose to give Doctor Strong good morning and he introduced me. "A new boy, Trotwood Copperfield."

The head boy stepped up to show me to my seat in such a polite way that I felt instantly less nervous. As I had little schooling for a long time, I truly felt like I was starting at the beginning. I was uneasy about that at first. I knew my life experiences were very strange compared to the other boys.

Still the boys were friendly and welcoming. Doctor Strong proved to be a kind master who expected the best of all his boys and was only very rarely disappointed. Plus, the quiet of Mr. Wickfield's house and the sweet company of Agnes soon made me the happiest of schoolboys.

Other than his lovely young wife and his school, Strong's great joy was creating a new dictionary, which he worked on constantly. In the years I went to school there, his dictionary seemed to come no closer to being finished. Many times I saw Strong walking around talking to himself with bits of paper sticking out of every pocket.

In all this time, I would have been the happiest of boys if it weren't for my growing dislike of Uriah Heep. The young man fawned over me whenever we met, which was as rarely as I could manage. He talked often about how very humble he was, but I sensed his remarks had layers of meaning I couldn't quite catch.

I wrote to Peggotty as soon as the whirlwind of change began to die down, and I was proud to repay the money she'd lent me. Though she was clearly happy for me to be safe and in a good situation, she still held my aunt in some awe. Several times she hinted that I would be quite welcome at Yarmouth if my aunt were to go alarmingly mad.

Peggotty said that Mr. Barkis had turned out to be an excellent husband, though still a bit overly careful with money. Mr. Peggotty was well, Ham was well, and Mrs. Gummidge was as gloomy as ever. Emily grew more lovely each day, though occasionally her longing for the life of a fine lady worried Peggotty.

Throughout my days at school, I went to Dover every third or fourth Saturday as a treat. And every alternate Wednesday, Mr. Dick came to visit me. He often brought his kite and was soon a great favorite among the boys at school.

One of the greatest surprises was how much Strong seemed to enjoy Mr. Dick's company. For a man whose family planned to shut him up in an asylum, Mr. Dick became quite a social success.

Somebody Turns Up

One day when I stepped out to walk, I heard a loud exclamation. "Copperfield? Is it possible?"

It was Mr. Micawber! I learned that Mr. Micawber was in exactly the same sort of situation as when I'd met him. He was deeply in debt and hounded by creditors, though he had avoided another trip to debtor's prison.

I was happy to spend a bit of time with the whole Micawber family. Soon, they caught a coach for London with hopes of finding fortune there.

After this, my school days passed one much like another. I fell deeply in love with one Miss Shepherd from Miss Nettingalls's School for

Girls. We were an impressive couple at the rare dances between our schools. Miss Shepherd grew tired of me eventually. I suffered terribly for it, but then healed. I moved up steadily in school and eventually became first boy.

Agnes Wickfield became my dearest friend and grew into a lady before my eyes, just as I grew from boy to young man. She seemed to make her passage with considerably more dignity than I made mine.

I fell madly in love with a Miss Larkin, who was several years my senior. This time I kept my affliction to myself and though I suffered again, I did it without Miss Larkin ever being aware of my devotion.

Finally my school days came to a close and I had no idea what to do next. My aunt suggested I might go on a small trip and look around to see if that produced a plan. So I took a somewhat sad leave of Agnes, my dearest and wisest friend, and began my trip.

My journey had barely begun before I ran into my old friend Steerforth at an inn at Charing Cross. I recognized him at once and called out, "Steerforth, won't you speak to me?"

He looked at me blankly for a moment, then shouted. "It's little Copperfield!"

We shook hands with such rejoicing that I had to wipe my eyes for the tears. Then he clapped me on the shoulder and demanded to

know the whole story of my life. I summed it up as quickly as I could and asked about him.

"I am what they call an Oxford man," he said. "Which means only that I get bored to death down there now and again. I am on my way to see my mother. You must come with me. You'll make the trip ever so much better." And so it was decided.

Steerforth's mother proved to be a proud woman who was clearly devoted to my friend. We stayed for several days and Mrs. Steerforth was polite to me for her son's sake. It wasn't long before Steerforth was eager to be moving again. He asked where I planned to go.

I told him I intended to visit dear friends in Yarmouth. He asked to come along and promptly charmed everyone there as soon as we arrived. We spent much of our time apart, as Steerforth often liked to ramble and meet people, while I preferred to spend my time with those I knew.

Though Peggotty didn't recognize me at first, I found her little changed. For the first time, I felt that I must have turned into a man while away at school.

I learned Mr. Barkis had given up carriage driving. He spent most of his time in bed, pained greatly by rheumatics. I found him so piled up with covers that he seemed only a face. He smiled at me when Peggotty announced me. Finally he said, "I was willin' a long time, sir?"

"A long time," I agreed.

"She's the best of women, Mrs. C.P. Barkis," he said. "All the praise that anyone can give to C.P. Barkis, she deserves and more!"

I agreed heartily.

I stayed for dinner and was delighted when Steerforth joined us. Afterward we walked out to visit at Mr. Peggotty's boat turned house.

Everyone was very taken with Steerforth. Miss Emily seemed quite shy of him at first, but I noticed her eyes rarely left him when Steerforth launched into tales of his travels.

"Emily has been like my own child," Mr. Peggoty said, turning our attention to her. "And I'm proud to say she's engaged to one who is iron-true to her. I know that no wrong can touch my Emily while that man lives."

I had only to take one glance at Ham to know who Emily's beloved was. Emily was clearly almost overcome by all the attention and fled the room. Eventually she was coaxed back and Steerforth managed to charm her into laughing again.

Steerforth and I finally left for the evening and made our way back into the small village.

"She is a most engaging beauty," Steerforth said when we talked about the evening. "But that's rather a chuckle-headed fellow for the girl."

I was startled by his reply until I guessed he must be making a joke. My friend would never be such a snob.

I Choose a Profession

Finally my trip drew to an end and I headed home. I had to admit, I still had no idea what profession I should choose. My aunt, however, had a suggestion.

"Would you like to be a proctor?" she asked.

I opened my eyes wide. "I imagine that would be an expensive profession to enter."

She waved away my worry. "If I have any object in life, it is to provide for your being a good, useful, and sensible man. We'll go to the Commons in the morning."

I knew that proctors acted much like lawyers in special court proceedings. I suspected there would be a great deal to learn, but I was excited by the idea.

I was to begin my profession and training at Spenlow and Jorkins in London. I soon learned that Mr. Jorkins rarely entered the offices and saw no one. Though his name was often thrown about whenever Mr. Spenlow needed a reason to disallow something.

"I would certainly be open to the idea," Mr. Spenlow would say, "but Mr. Jorkins has his opinions on these matters and I am bound to respect that."

When I finally met Mr. Jorkins, I found him the mildest of men who seemed unlikely to hold firm opinions about anything.

After securing my post, I needed a place to stay. My aunt found a set of furnished rooms advertised in the newspaper. I liked the idea of my own place and soon secured them.

My time with Spenlow and Jorkins passed in something of a blur. I had a great deal to learn but soon showed a talent for the complicated twistings of the law.

Though my time was vastly taken up, I found I could still manage a visit now and then to my dear friend Agnes. She was more like a sister to me on every meeting and always gave me the best advice.

The only unpleasant thing to mar our visits was my notice that Uriah Heep seemed to have grown in his status with the law firm. Sometimes it was as though he ran the firm and not Mr. Wickfield.

"I do beg you, Trotwood," Agnes said. "Be friendly to Uriah. Don't resent what may be unpleasant about him. Think of Papa."

I didn't understand why it was important to her, but I agreed. When I had the unfortunate opportunity to be in the presence of Heep, I did my best to remain civil. He had a highly distasteful way of referring to Agnes that made me want to thump him, but I refrained.

"Oh Master Copperfield!" he gushed on one such meeting. "With what a pure affection do I love the ground my Agnes walks on!"

I had the urge to run him through with a red-hot poker from the nearby fireplace. Only reminding myself that Agnes was as sensible as she was kind kept me from doing something rash. I was certain she would never entertain affection for someone like Heep.

As I continued to grow more knowledgeable about the law, something even more agreeable caught my attention. Mr. Spenlow had a charming daughter named Dora, and I fell in love with her at our first meeting. She had bright eyes and a head full of curls.

I was so blinded by my instant love that I had not yet noticed the older woman who stood behind her. "I have seen Mr. Copperfield before," a cold voice noted.

I looked right into the face of Miss Murdstone, Dora's hired companion and chaperone. When a quiet moment presented itself, Miss Murdstone suggested we not mention the past. I was happy to oblige.

From the first moment I saw Dora, I began coming up with any excuse to see her again. I would go walking far out of my way to pass her house. Sometimes I would see her at a distance. Sometimes I would not see her at all. And sometimes she would be close enough to walk a bit with me.

Whenever I saw her, she carried around a small dog named Jip. The little dog would growl at me jealously every time I stepped close.

"It's so stupid at home," she complained. "Miss Murdstone is ridiculous and only lets me outside when I need to be aired!" Then she laughed and I am certain I heard music in it. "She scolded about today though and said the weather would not be good for me. I had to insist to Papa."

"The day did seem very dark to me," I said. "And now it seems truly bright."

"Is that a compliment?" she asked. "Or has the weather really changed?"

I stammered a bit and managed a foolish sounding compliment. She blushed and hid behind her curls. Then she flitted off onto a fresh subject.

"Miss Murdstone is so very cross, isn't she, Jip?" she asked the little dog, and he answered with a bark. "We make ourselves as happy as we can though, just to spite her."

Every bit of talk I managed with Dora simply cast me deeper in love. I was the most hopeless creature alive.

A Loss

During my few social functions, I made an amazing discovery. My old friend Tommy Traddles was now a solicitor in London. I set out one afternoon after work to find him.

The street was a shabby one and reminded me of living with Mr. and Mrs. Micawber. I was reminded still stronger of my past as I listened to a young maid argue with the milkman about his bill.

The maid let me in cheerfully enough and I climbed a long set of stairs to Tommy's room. His rooms were small and fairly stuffed with things. His delight in seeing me was clear. We talked about old times for a while, then moved on to sweethearts. Tommy was engaged to a curate's daughter, though they had no set date for their eventual wedding.

I was quite jealous as I longed for nothing more than to be engaged to Dora Spenlow.

"My Sophie is such a dear girl!" Traddles said of his beloved. "We've already made a beginning toward housekeeping and have two pieces of furniture." He proudly showed off the flowerpot and stand that Sophie had bought and a small round table with a marble top that he had purchased. I praised them both.

Eventually, we got around to a topic that surprised me greatly. He was boarding with none other than Mr. and Mrs. Micawber! We had a grand reunion as soon as Tommy learned that I knew them.

I found the dear couple in terrible financial straits, as always. Mrs. Micawber had a great plan for them to find their way out though. They would advertise in the newspapers! She was certain an ad listing all of Mr. Micawber's fine qualities would soon get them the perfect position. I wished them well.

Before I left, I took Traddles aside and cautioned him against loaning money to the Micawbers. The look on his face made me suspect I was too late.

Not long after my visit to Traddles, I ran into Steerforth again. He had been visiting in Yarmouth and had bad news for me. Mr. Barkis was near death. I left the city immediately.

I found Mr. Peggotty and Emily keeping Peggotty company. Emily was very pale and quiet. I was touched by how deeply she seemed moved by the soon passing of Mr. Barkis. Peggotty urged me up the stairs.

"Barkis, my dear," Peggotty said, almost cheerfully. "Here's Master Davy."

Mr. Barkis dragged his eyes open and murmured softly about driving me to school.

"Barkis, my dear," Peggotty said.

"C.P. Barkis," he whispered. "No better woman anywhere." Then he turned his faded eyes to me and smiled. "Barkis is willing." With those soft words, he died.

I stayed a time with Peggotty as she dealt with all the details of funeral and inheritance. It seemed that Mr. Barkis had left her quite a bit of money in a small chest. My dearest Peggotty would never need to work again.

One evening, we gathered at Mr. Peggotty's boathouse. The house looked just as I remembered and Mrs. Gummidge was as gloomy as ever.

"Cheer up, my pretty mawther," Mr. Peggotty said. "Cheer up and see if a good deal more doesn't come natural."

"Not to me, Daniel," she groaned. "Only thing natural to me is to be lone and lorn."

"Where's Emily?" Mr. Peggotty wondered. "It's not like Ham to be so slow walking her home." Finally we heard footsteps outside and Mr. Peggotty clapped. "Here she is!"

It was only Ham. He asked me to step out a moment with him. I saw then that he was deathly pale. "Ham!" I cried. "What's the matter?"

At that, he broke down and wept. Finally, he choked out a few scant details. Emily was gone. She'd run away with Steerforth. I took the news like a blow. I had brought Steerforth into this place. How could he have done such a thing?

Emily had left a note saying she would never return unless Steerforth brought her back a lady. I knew there was no chance that Steerforth would marry a girl from a lower social class. He would break Emily's heart, but he would not marry her. Finally, Ham and I went together into the small house and broke the news to the family.

Mr. Peggotty uttered no cry and shed no tear. He simply vowed to find her. "I will seek my niece through the world. I'll bring her home. Once she sees me, she'll come," he said firmly. "I know she will."

My Aunt Astonishes Me

Mr. Peggotty was as good as his word. He traveled greatly. I saw him now and again as he passed through London. He never wavered and never doubted that he would find his niece.

I finally received word through Steerforth's family that he had abandoned Emily in Italy. He'd grown tired of her sadness over leaving her family. No one knew where she went after that, but I felt certain she would return to London eventually. Mr. Peggotty kept up the search.

Meanwhile, two tremendous things happened in my own affairs. The first I learned about from an unexpected visit from my aunt. In her no-nonsense way, she announced, "I am ruined, my dear! All I have in the world is in this trunk I have brought with me. I will sell the cottage, of course, but I hoped I might stay with you until that happens."

I said she must stay as long as she wished. She could have my bed. Then I asked how such a thing could happen. She vaguely mentioned some business reverses.

I immediately began a search for higher-paying work so that I might support us both. Even Mr. Dick found work with the help of dear Tommy Traddles. Mr. Dick had fine, clear handwriting and Traddles set him to work copying legal documents. Mr. Dick took to the work proudly.

I discovered my dear schoolmaster was looking for a secretary to help with the dictionary. I hurried to see him and was given the job immediately. I would work for Doctor Strong in the mornings before I went in to the proctor's office. Then, I would return in the afternoons after I was done.

I also bought some books on shorthand and I studied late into every night until I mastered the form. This allowed me to get work writing court transcripts. Looking back, it is amazing how much work I fit into each day, but I felt extremely happy to be able to support myself and my kind aunt.

When I tried to explain to Dora that I was quite poor now, she merely laughed at me and insisted I shouldn't talk about such sad things or she would have Jip bite me. I did ask if she could love me still and she insisted she could.

"You're very naughty to even ask," she said.

The one hardship to our love was Miss Murdstone. She carried word of our growing affection to Dora's father. Mr. Spenlow called me into his office to tell me directly that his daughter would not be marrying me.

"Have you considered her station in life and the plans I might have for her advancement?" he asked.

I bowed my head. "No, sir," I admitted. "I have only considered how much I love her."

He shook his head. "Don't talk to me about love. And don't talk to my daughter about it either. I may have to send her abroad again to get such silly notions out of her head."

I was heartbroken that I had not gone about my relationship with Dora in a manner to please her father. I had only meant to avoid the loathsome Miss Murdstone, but clearly I had seemed sneaky to Mr. Spenlow. I was certain that my life was over.

Then the most amazing thing happened. The morning after my confrontation with Mr. Spenlow, I went straight to the Commons. I was surprised to see a crowd around the office. Inside, the clerks were there but no one was doing anything.

"This is a dreadful calamity, Mr. Copperfield," said the oldest of the clerks.

"What is?" I asked.

"Mr. Spenlow," he whispered. "Dead!"

The office spun around me at this announcement. I would have fainted if one of the clerks had not caught my arm and led me to a chair. Mr. Spenlow had taken his small coach out by himself and the coach had arrived home without him. They found Mr. Spenlow a mile from the house. He lay in the road, quite dead.

I learned that Mr. Spenlow was actually poorer than anyone had suspected. Miss Murdstone was dismissed. Dora was penniless and would be moving in with two elderly aunts. She was allowed to bring along a dear friend to comfort her, Miss Julia Mills. Miss Mills was a romantic creature and often sent me notes to let me know how Dora was recovering.

I really felt quite at a loss, so I turned to my truest friend and helper, Agnes. I knew she would know best how to handle the situation. When I reached Mr. Wickfield's, I was shocked to have Mr. Micawber answer the door.

It seemed he had gone through with Mrs. Micawber's grand idea of advertising his abilities. He had been offered a job by Uriah Heep. Mr. Micawber seemed more stressed now than he ever had when jobless and in debt.

"Do you see much of Mr. Wickfield?" I asked.

"Not much," Mr. Micawber said and then lowered his voice. "It would be best for me if I didn't talk at all about the business."

I assured him that would be fine. I soon excused myself and headed up to see Agnes. I learned that Mrs. Heep now lived with the Wickfields and cast a gloom over the family as dark as old Mrs. Gummidge ever did over the Peggottys. But Agnes still greeted me with sweetness and warmth.

I poured out my concerns about Dora. Agnes, as always, had excellent advice. "The honorable course is to write to those two ladies, Dora's aunts. Relate as plainly and openly as possible what has happened. Tell them you will abide by any conditions they might set." She looked me over solemnly. "Try not to be too emotional."

"What if they say no?" I moaned.

"I don't think I would consider that," Agnes said. "Only ask yourself what is the right and honorable thing to do. Then do that."

I realized she was right. I felt a weight lift from me. But my good feeling would not last, for evening came and so did dinner.

I found Uriah Heep and his mother now dined with the family. I did not like the way Heep watched every move Agnes made. After dinner, the women retired from the room and Heep encouraged Mr. Wickfield with glass after glass of wine.

Finally, Heep raised a glass and proposed a toast. "To Agnes," he said, "the divinest of her sex." Then he grinned craftily. "To be her father is a proud distinction, I am sure, but to be her husband—"

Mr. Wickfield cried out as if in pain.

"What's the matter?" Heep demanded, his face turning a deadly color. "If I say I have an ambition to make your Agnes my Agnes, I have as good a right as another man. I have a better right!"

I put my arm around Mr. Wickfield and begged him to calm himself. "He is the millstone around my neck," Mr. Wickfield said. "He has power over me because of my weakness. But surely I have not done such a thing to my own daughter."

At his wails, Agnes burst into the room and led her father out. He laid his head on her shoulder and followed.

"Ah, I was a bit too soon," Heep said. "It'll ripen."

Heep shuffled out and I sat up worrying about my dear old friends. Finally, Agnes joined me in the common rooms and I related what had happened.

"You'll never sacrifice yourself to such a mistaken sense of duty, will you?" I asked.

"You need have no such fear for me," she said firmly.

CHAPTER 15

Dora's Aunts

As always, the advice I had gotten from Agnes was excellent. I visited Dora many times at the Spenlow sisters' home.

The old ladies treated Dora like a pet and spoiled her as completely as her father ever had. She slowly grew out of her sadness over her father and seemed happy to see me again.

The Spenlow aunts made it quite clear they would be comfortable with Dora marrying me as soon as my situation would allow. So I doubled my efforts to make money for us.

I had to admit we would never be rich. So, I thought it might be helpful for Dora to learn a bit of cooking and how to keep the home accounts.

"Why are you so cruel?" she asked when it was clear neither would come easily to her. "Don't find fault with me, Doady," she said. "And I'll be good."

What could I do but kiss away her tears and tell her how I doted on her? Eventually she did find a use for the cookbook. She taught Jip to sit on it and clapped happily about the trick.

I continued to study stenography until I mastered it and was able to make a respectable income from it. I soon began recording the debates of Parliament for the morning newspaper. I saw the true worth of political life. It is a life of words and not of deeds.

My success with the newspapers gave me the confidence to try my hand at authorship. I had a little something published in a magazine. Then I wrote more and more, until I was regularly paid for this as well.

I moved from the Buckingham Street rooms to a pleasant little cottage. My aunt purchased a tiny cottage close to mine as she had sold her old house. I reached twenty-one years old. So with a home, a steady income, and the blessings of adulthood, I was ready for marriage.

The Spenlow aunts gave their consent and threw themselves into plans for the wedding. They also found furniture for Dora and I to look at. Dora had little interest, though she did insist upon the purchase of a Chinese house for Jip with little bells on the top.

Traddles brought his dear Sophie to the wedding. They were still waiting for improvement so that they might be married. Agnes came from Canterbury and soon became a great favorite of Dora and Sophie. Peggotty joined us, of course, as well as my aunt and Mr. Dick.

"My own boy could never be dearer than you," Aunt Betsey told me. Then she gave me a kiss.

At the church, Agnes stood at Dora's side, for my bride was trembling like a leaf in the wind. The ceremony itself passed in a blur.

We headed home together and my dear wife said, "Are you happy now, you foolish boy? Are you sure you don't repent?"

I had no wish for anything different then, but we soon ran into difficulties. It seemed every tradesman in London had heard of us and made it a point to cheat us. We went through a long parade of servants, each leaving with more of our belongings than the one before. I coaxed Dora to be a bit firmer with the servants so that they would feel less comfortable with stealing our things.

"Oh no, please," she said. "I am such a little goose and they know it. Oh, don't scold me any more."

"No scolding," I said. "I only want to reason."

She wrinkled her nose. "Reasoning is worse than scolding. You must be sorry that you married me or you wouldn't reason with me!"

Finally we simply accepted that it would continue to be far more expensive for us to live than any other family. My wife was happy when I was happy and distraught whenever I showed the slightest sign of seriousness.

In the evening when I worked on my stories, she sat beside me and held my pens. Nothing delighted her more than when I asked for a new pen and she could give it to me promptly. I worried that it was a dull pursuit for her, but she begged me not to make her do anything else.

"Let me always stop and see you write," she said. "You're such a naturally clever boy. I'm not clever at all."

At that I laughed and said, "It's better to be naturally Dora than anything else in the world."

She shook her head, turned her delighted bright eyes up to mine, kissed me, broke into a merry laugh, and sprang away to set Jip to a few tricks.

When I accepted Dora as herself, our lives fell into a comfortable and happy rhythm. Our second year of marriage was even happier than our first. For a time, it seemed as though we might add a child to our family but it was not to be. And the attempt to carry a baby left Dora weak and unwell.

"When I can run about again, as I used to do," she told my aunt one day, "I shall make Jip race. He is getting quite slow and lazy."

"I suspect, my blossom," Aunt Betsey said, "that he is simply getting old."

Dora stroked his soft ears. "Oh, poor fellow."

"I think he'll last a good time yet," my aunt said. "But quietly."

Each day, Dora seemed to grow weaker instead of stronger. I began to carry her downstairs every morning and upstairs every night. She would put her arms around my neck and laugh.

My aunt and Mr. Dick carried piles of pillows and blankets to settle her comfortably. Many nights passed when I would lay my head down and cry to think of how my wife grew lighter on each trip.

Intelligence

One evening, I received the oddest note from Mr. Micawber asking if I would bring Traddles to a meeting with him. He seemed very distressed about some mysterious problem.

I read the note several times. Even though I knew Mr. Micawber was a great fan of dramatic notes, I suspected something serious might be behind this one.

I met with Traddles and soon learned that he had received a note from Mrs. Micawber, who feared her husband was involved in something illegal. We decided to meet with Mr. Micawber as soon as possible.

"I am crushed under the misery and cruelty of Heep," Mr. Micawber lamented. "He had sucked me into fraud, conspiracy, deception. All that is evil is Heep!"

We tried to comfort Mr. Micawber, as he seemed on the verge of some kind of nervous collapse. "I must do the right thing," he insisted. "It will put me in prison. Oh, my poor darling wife. How she has suffered because of Heep! I will expose the ruffian. I must!"

At that, he rushed away from us, leaving us more confused than before. This meeting was followed by a series of notes and meetings. A plan was made for ending the connection between Uriah Heep and Mr. Wickfield.

But before that severance could occur, another surprising event broke in. Mr. Peggotty found Emily! She had returned to London after the cruel desertion of Steerforth. She had not had the courage to go home, but Mr. Peggotty found her on the streets before anything more horrible could happen.

Mr. Peggotty sent word that he would be taking Emily with him to start a new life in

Australia, along with Mrs. Gummidge! The lone woman had made a complete change and now stood ready to help in any way she could.

I was amazed to think how much people could change and how little we can guess about the journey of life. Who would have thought that Emily would go through such a painful journey, then find her way back to an uncle who loved her? Who would have thought that Mr. Micawber might find himself in the place of hero? Yet, these things happened.

When the day came for springing Mr. Micawber's trap, I was quite divided on what I should do. Mr. Micawber wished my aunt and Mr. Dick to be there. I did not like to leave my dear Dora alone.

"You must go or I won't speak to you again," Dora told us sternly. "I'll be disagreeable. I'll make Jip bark at you. I shall call you cross old things if you don't go."

"Tut, Blossom," Aunt Betsey said. "How will you do without us?"

"I can stay upstairs while you are gone and look after myself quite well," she said.

And so we agreed because we couldn't imagine defying our Dora.

The next day, a fine group of us headed off to our meeting. My aunt tied the strings of her bonnet with a resolute air. Traddles buttoned his coat with the determination of a man heading to war. Mr. Dick even pulled his hat on more tightly.

Mr. Micawber met us on the street. "Gentlemen and madam," he said, "good morning."

Mr. Dick greeted him with such enthusiastic handshaking that my aunt had to step in to retrieve the man's hand.

"What would you have us do?" I asked Mr. Micawber.

"Wait five minutes for me to do a small chore," he said. "Then ask for Miss Wickfield at the office of Wickfield and Heep. I have no more to say at the present."

We waited the allotted time before heading into the offices, where we found Mr. Micawber at his desk. "How do you do, Mr. Micawber," I said formally. "Is Miss Wickfield at home?"

He led us up the stairs and announced us in a formal voice. We found Heep alone in the upstairs rooms and greeted him stiffly. Then dear Agnes came in and Heep waved at Mr. Micawber. "You may go."

"I think not," said Mr. Micawber.

"Go along," Heep insisted, glaring. "I will talk to you presently."

"I will talk about you now," Mr. Micawber said. At that, he launched into a list of the illegal things he had been asked to do by Heep. To that list, he added the things Heep had done on his own without Mr. Micawber's aid.

"That won't do!" Heep shouted.

"I have proof that Heep forged Mr. Wickfield's signature many times. He made it appear that Mr. Wickfield had lost his client's money," Mr. Micawber said. "In fact, Mr. Heep

placed those funds into his own accounts. I have the books for those accounts."

Heep turned very pale and rushed to a desk nearby, opening a drawer with a small key. Then he wailed to find the drawer empty.

"I have turned over all the books to Mr. Traddles. I know I may go to prison for my part in these horrible activities, but I will do so with a clear conscience and sure knowledge that I have ruined Mr. Uriah Heep!"

"You stole the books!" Heep shouted at Traddles.

"No," Traddles said. "I have Mr. Wickfield's legal power of attorney. And I will be looking into his affairs that I might get them in proper order."

"What do you want from me?" Heep asked.

My aunt stalked over to Heep and glared into his face. "I want my property! I was willing to let it go when I thought it was Mr. Wickfield's error. But I will not give my money to you, Heep."

"You will turn over all the money you stole," Traddles said. "You will no longer be a partner of Mr. Wickfield. And you will most likely go to jail."

This was the end of the tyranny of Mr. Uriah Heep. After this, Mr. Wickfield recovered slowly under the kind attention of Agnes. Mr. Micawber was arrested a few times for small debts he owed to Heep. At each arrest, one of us would pay the money and Mr. Micawber would be free again.

Finally, the Micawbers thought it would be best for them to make a fresh start. They decided to travel to Australia on the exact same ship as Mr. Peggotty and Emily.

Chapter 17

The New Wound

Back in Yarmouth, Ham had become quite a hero to his neighbors since Emily left. It seemed there was no job too dangerous for Ham. I had my suspicions about what drove the young man to his heroic actions, but I kept them to myself.

The day before the ship was to sail for Australia, I received horrifying news. A terrible storm had struck Yarmouth just days after Mrs. Gummidge left to join Mr. Peggotty and Emily for the voyage. The villagers rushed to the shore. They knew such a terrible storm could swamp boats and cause shipwrecks.

This storm was worse than any could remember. A small ship was caught in the pounding sea that drove it relentlessly toward the rocks of the shoreline. The villagers watched in horror as waves passed over the decks again and again, washing away sailors.

Finally the last three men on the ship lashed themselves to the mast, but even that could not save them. A massive wave passed over the ship and then there was just one man left aboard.

The waves drove the ship onto the rocks not far from shore. In the pounding sea, no one could get out to the boat, though everyone could see the young man battered again and again as the waves rushed over the rails.

Ham insisted that he would swim out to the ship and get the young sailor. The villagers tied a stout rope to his middle and all the men held the end. The sea could not take Ham away, but the pounding was too much even for the strong young shipbuilder. Ham drowned and the villagers dragged his limp body to shore.

The sea broke up the small ship and killed the young sailor as well. When his body washed ashore, it was identified by papers carried in his coat pockets. The young sailor was Steerforth.

I couldn't bear to tell Mr. Peggotty and Emily. I could see hope for the first time on Emily's face. I couldn't put out that small light. They would know soon enough, so I joined the crowd of well wishers and saw the ship leave. I hoped Australia would bring each of them what they most needed.

I wish that the passing of the young man I had so admired as a child and the strong hero with the lion's heart were the last deaths I knew, but that was not to be. My own dear Dora grew thinner and thinner. She asked me to send for Agnes so they might visit.

"I was too young to be a very good wife," Dora told me on the night of Agnes's visit.

"We have been very happy, my sweet Dora," I said.

"I was very happy, very," she said softly. "But I am glad you haven't had time to grow tired of such a silly child wife."

"Never," I said. "I will always love you."

She kissed me. "And I love you. It is the only thing of value I have except being pretty. Remember always that I could not have been loved better than I was by you. Now, go downstairs a bit and let me visit with Agnes again."

I walked down and sat by the fire. Jip crawled out of his house and looked at me. He licked my hand and lifted his dim eyes to my face. I rubbed his ears, still soft despite the gray in his coat. Then he stretched himself out as if to sleep and with a small cry, he died.

I stood and looked toward the stairs where Agnes was coming down. What would I tell Dora about Jip? She was so very weak. Then I saw the tears and grief on Agnes's face.

"Agnes?" I said just before I fainted.

A Light Shines

I traveled for years after the death of my dear wife. Sadness lay on me so heavily that it seemed my heart could barely beat. I continued to write and my books were published. My fame grew but I cared little.

I ended up in Switzerland. The incredible beauty of the place began my healing, so I stayed. I wrote. I took long walks and my health grew robust even as my heart slowly mended.

I received a packet of letters from Agnes when I had stopped moving long enough for them to catch me. Her words were as wise and bright as ever.

I marveled at her belief in me. She had absolute faith that I would come out on the other side of grief and that I would do great things. How could anyone who knew me so well always think so well of me?

I read her letters many times. I wrote to her. I told her that without her I never would be what she seemed to think I was. I said she inspired me to try.

I thought long and often of Agnes and suddenly I saw something with clear eyes. I loved Agnes and I believed she loved me. But I had so long built up the relationship of brother and sister between us that I doubted we could ever be more than that.

I went home to London. My first visit was to Tommy Traddles. I learned he had finally married while I was gone. Now he lived with Sophie and her sisters. I had never seen Traddles so completely content, even though his rooms were crowded with giggling women. I was cheered by his happiness.

My next stop was to see my aunt. She told me that she heard often from the Micawbers and that they had taken to the simple life of Australia with vigor. Mr. Micawber had become a man of some note now and his success had allowed him to settle every past debt.

I learned that Mr. Dick continued with his occupation as a copier and delighted in being able to support himself.

Finally I touched on the subject of Agnes. I said I intended to visit her and her father the next day.

"Mr. Wickfield no longer practices law," my aunt said. "Agnes has opened a school for girls, I believe it is a great success."

"How could it be otherwise?" I asked. "Does she have anyone special in her life?"

My aunt smiled. "She could have married twenty times, my dear, since you have been gone. I suspect she has a grand love of her life and I believe she is going to be married. But those are only my thoughts and you should not repeat them."

"If Agnes is in love," I said, "I am certain she will tell me."

So I went the next day to Canterbury and my heart soared at the sight of my dear Agnes. It was my intention to keep my feelings secret, but I had never been able to keep a secret from Agnes.

"You are so thoughtful," Agnes said.

"Shall I tell you why?" I asked.

Agnes peered at me, her face anxious for the first time.

"Dearest Agnes, I respect you and honor you and I love you," I said. "I wish only that I could call you something more than friend, more even than sister."

At that Agnes began to cry and I stared at her tears in horror. "Agnes, even when I loved Dora, I counted so much on you. I would be lost without you. I went away loving you, though I did not see it yet. I stayed away loving you. I returned home loving you."

She laid a gentle hand on my arm and said softly, "I have loved you all my life."

And so, my life changed again. Agnes and I were married and two happier people could hardly have lived.

We had children of our own and lived our lives in the happiness of dear friends and family. What more could any man ask?